RECEIVED

D0538292

D LIBRARY

NO LONGER PROPERTY OF
SEATTLE PUBLIC LIBRARY

BOOK'S BIG ADVENTURE

For our beloved librarians, who help match readers to great books.
—A. L.

For Christina A. Tugeau, Christy Ewers, and Laurent Linn,
who light the world with books. Thank you for believing in me.
—R. J. B.

SIMON & SCHUSTER BOOKS FOR YOUNG READERS
An imprint of Simon & Schuster Children's Publishing Division
1230 Avenue of the Americas, New York, New York 10020
Text © 2021 by Adam Lehrhaupt
Illustration © 2021 by Rahele Jomepour Bell
Book design by Laurent Linn © 2021 by Simon & Schuster, Inc.
All rights reserved, including the right of reproduction in whole or in part in any form.
SIMON & SCHUSTER BOOKS FOR YOUNG READERS and related marks are trademarks of Simon & Schuster, Inc.
For information about special discounts for bulk purchases,
please contact Simon & Schuster Special Sales at 1-866-506-1949 or business@simonandschuster.com.
The Simon & Schuster Speakers Bureau can bring authors to your live event. For more information or to book an event,
contact the Simon & Schuster Speakers Bureau at 1-866-248-3049 or visit our website at www.simonspeakers.com.
The text for this book was set in Cabrito.
The illustrations for this book were rendered using digital brushes and scanned, hand-printed textures.
Manufactured in China
1120 SCP
First Edition
2 4 6 8 10 9 7 5 3 1
Library of Congress Cataloging-in-Publication Data
Names: Lehrhaupt, Adam, author. | Bell, Rahele Jomepour, illustrator.
Title: Book's big adventure / Adam Lehrhaupt ; illustrated by Rahele Jomepour Bell.
Description: First edition. | New York : Simon & Schuster Books for Young Readers/A Paula Wiseman Book, [2021] | "A Paula Wiseman Book." |
Audience: Ages 4-8. | Audience: Grades 2-3. | Summary: When Book was new, it had many exciting adventures but over time,
it leaves the library less and less often until, at last, it is given away and begins again.
Identifiers: LCCN 2020029320 (print) | LCCN 2020029321 (ebook) |
ISBN 9781534421837 (hardcover) | ISBN 9781534421844 (ebook)
Subjects: CYAC: Books—Fiction.
Classification: LCC PZ7.L532745 Boo 2021 (print) | LCC PZ7.L532745 (ebook) | DDC [E]—dc23
LC record available at https://lccn.loc.gov/2020029320
LC ebook record available at https://lccn.loc.gov/2020029321

BOOK'S BIG ADVENTURE

WRITTEN BY
Adam Lehrhaupt

ILLUSTRATED BY
Rahele Jomepour Bell

A PAULA WISEMAN BOOK
SIMON & SCHUSTER BOOKS FOR YOUNG READERS
NEW YORK LONDON TORONTO SYDNEY NEW DELHI

Book was new.

The cover bright and shiny.

Its home a prominent shelf.

Book had many adventures.

In a car.

At a picnic.

During bedtime.

Book was happy.

One day, Book was moved to a different shelf.

A lower, less friendly shelf.

Over time, Book's cover faded.

The title grew hard to read.

BOOKS
FOR

BOOKS
FOR
DONATION

BOOKS

Book went on
fewer and fewer
adventures.

Day after day,
Book sat on the new shelf.

THE BOOK

It watched as other books arrived . . .

and left . . .

on adventures of their own.

Book was lonely.

Forgotten.

It wondered if its travels were over.

It longed for one last adventure.

But Book's cover didn't have bright pictures
of knights
or princesses,
fancy cars,
or fast trains.

So no one noticed it.

Book sat on its shelf.

Longing.

Wishing.

Until . . .

It was bumped.

It tumbled.

There it sat.

Day after day.

No one found it.

Book began to lose hope.

One night, a light slashed
through the darkness.

A kind face leaned in.

Book was picked up.

Dusted off.

Read.

Book felt hope pour through its pages.

Was this it? The next big adventure?

But then Book was dropped.

Covered.

And there it lay.

Silent.

Sad.

This wasn't a fun adventure.

Book was about to give up,

when . . .

Suddenly, Book was chosen again.

Given.

Received.

Loved.

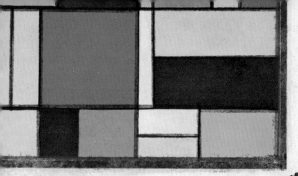

Book went on *many* new adventures.

To a museum.

To a basketball court.

Even to Book's favorite—a classroom.

Book was given a brand-new home.

And Book was very, very happy.

AUTHOR'S NOTE

I have a huge collection of books. So many that some of them live in boxes instead of on their shelves. That's no place for a book to live.

One day, I was visiting a school to talk to the students, and I asked the librarian what happens to the books they don't have space for anymore. She told me a wonderful story about how her school donates the excess books each summer to readers who don't have big book collections of their own.

I loved this idea. Not only would it help give new life to my beloved books, but it would let new readers develop their own attachment to them. I dove right in to figure out where I could send my collection.

It turns out there are A LOT of places that are looking for book donations. Lucky for you, I've already done the research. With that said, this list is by no means complete. There are many smaller local organizations that your school, library, or community center can tell you about. Just ask!

BOOK DONATION IDEAS

Women's shelters—These shelters provide a safe space for women and their children. Books are the perfect distraction and can be a bright light in a difficult time.

Little Free Library—These libraries can be found in neighborhoods all over the country. Readers can take and return books as they please. You can add your books to an existing site or build your own. Doesn't that sound like fun? **littlefreelibrary.org**

Kids Need to Read and **Reader to Reader**—These organizations provide books to schools, libraries, and literacy programs for communities that are most in need, including inner-city schools, Native American reservations, small rural towns, and many more. Sounds like the kind of place your books would love to visit. **kidsneedtoread.org / readertoreader.org**

The Salvation Army—Established in 1865 and helping in 130 countries around the world, this organization provides books for disaster relief and homeless shelters as well as much more. Your books can find great happiness here. **satruck.org/dropoff**

Goodwill—This nonprofit accepts book donations for their resale stores. Proceeds from these stores fund training and programs to help people overcome challenges to build skills, find jobs, and grow their careers. Imagine all the good your books can do here. **goodwill.org**

Books for Africa and the **African Library Project**—These organizations are working toward ending the cycle of poverty and illiteracy in Africa. Their books are used to create school libraries and literacy programs. I bet your books would love to go on this amazing trip. **booksforafrica.org / africanlibraryproject.org**